My   My teddy bear at home

c.1   13.95

DATE DUE			

D1064869

★ A YOUNG READERS TITLE ★

MY · TEDDY · BEAR

AT HOME

For a free color catalog describing Gareth Stevens' list of high-quality books, call 1-800-542-2595 (USA) or 1-800-461-9120 (Canada). Gareth Stevens' Fax: (414) 225-0377.

Library of Congress Cataloging-in-Publication Data

My teddy bear at home / by Irwin Jorvik, Ltd.; illustrated by
   Anthony Fletcher
       p. cm. -- (My teddy bear)
    "First published in Great Britain in 1993 by Kibworth Books,
Imperial Road, Kibworth Beauchamp"--T.p. verso.
    Summary: Teddy Bear fears that his friends will not remember
his birthday, but the toy friends have planned a surprise party with
treats and gifts.
    ISBN 0-8368-1536-X (lib. bdg.)
    [1. Teddy Bears--Fiction. 2. Toys--Fiction. 3. Birthdays-
-Fiction. 4. Parties--Fiction.] I. Fletcher, Anthony, 1965- ill.
II. Irwin Jorvik, Ltd. III. Series.
PZ7.M97855 1996
[E]--dc20   95-36325

This edition first published in North America in 1996 by
Gareth Stevens Publishing
1555 North RiverCenter Drive, Suite 201
Milwaukee, Wisconsin 53212, USA

First published in Great Britain in 1993 by Kibworth Books, Imperial Road, Kibworth Beauchamp. Text and compilation © 1993 by Irwin Jorvik Ltd. Illustrations © 1993 by Anthony Fletcher.

Printed in the United States of America

1 2 3 4 5 6 7 8 9 99 98 97 96

A YOUNG READERS TITLE

MY·TEDDY·BEAR

AT HOME

Gareth Stevens Publishing
MILWAUKEE

Teddy Bear is waiting for his friends to arrive. They have promised to come for a visit today. Teddy hopes they remember that it is a special day for a little bear. He is very excited; maybe he will even get some presents.

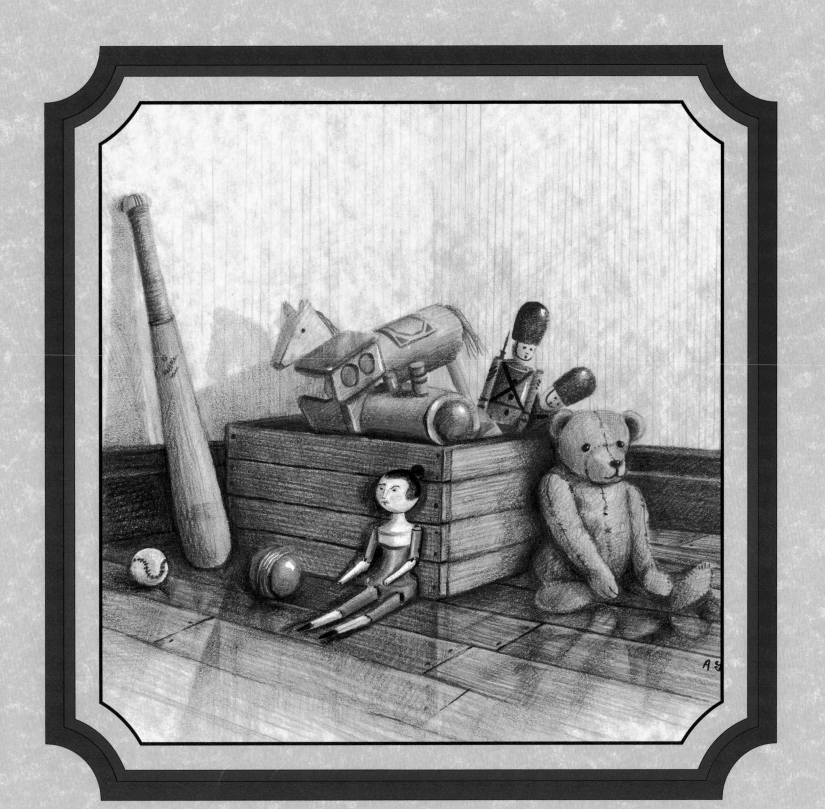

Teddy has to clean his room first. His clothes are scattered all over the floor. One by one, he picks them up and puts them in the closet. Oh dear, Teddy Bear has lost his socks. "Here they are behind the clock," laughs his friend Clown, who has just arrived with Wooden Duck.

"Can we help?" they ask.

Wooden Duck helps Rag Rabbit make Teddy Bear's bed. Wooden Duck has found some clean sheets and a blanket in the dresser. Making the bed is very hard work. At last it is done, except there is a funny bump right in the middle! What is it? Wooden Duck suddenly remembers they have left the pillow under the sheets and will have to start over again!

Wooden Doll is downstairs sweeping the floor with a big broom. There are lots of crumbs under the table, and she even finds Teddy Bear's watch. He is always losing his belongings. Although he is happy she has found it, Teddy also feels disappointed. Nobody has remembered that today is a special day.

Picking up a dust cloth, Teddy begins to dust the mirror and shelves. He has to stretch up high to reach everything, and he nearly knocks over the goldfish bowl. There are lots of treasures to dust, and he thinks he will never finish.

Rag Elephant helps by watering a large plant. It's very thirsty. The plant has not been watered for a long time, so Rag Elephant uses his long trunk to help with the job. But while all this activity is going on, Wooden Doll and Clown are preparing a surprise for Teddy.

15

Happy Birthday, Teddy! The toys came to help him clean his house, but they also came to set up Teddy Bear's surprise party with balloons and streamers and a magnificent cake. Teddy Bear is so happy. His friends didn't forget his birthday after all.

There are lots of dirty dishes to wash before the toys can play games. Teddy Bear washes all of the bowls, mugs, plates, and spoons. His friends dry the dishes and put them away. Wooden Doll is in charge of making sure they all do their jobs properly.

19

Now that the kitchen is clean and all the dishes are put away, the toys go up to the playroom. Teddy Bear rides his rocking horse, which he has named *Picnic*. After they play some games together, Teddy's friends must go home because it is getting late. It has been a wonderful day.

Teddy Bear enjoyed the day so much. He thought everybody had forgotten his birthday, but it turned out to be the best ever. He got a new tennis racket, a ball, and a shiny new sailboat. As the day ends, he plans his next adventure — he and his friends will take the boat to the shallow lake in the park.